I would like to thank all those who made my second book, Oh No! There's a Bully in Our School!!!, *a huge success. Also, a very special thank you to my family, friends, teachers, students, organizations, and colleagues, who have provided me with the motivation, support, and encouragement to write this book. I'm appreciative of all of you for pushing me to be a great author. Because you all are behind me every step of the way along the path guiding me through my career as an author, there's no doubt that I'll be able to continue to inspire children around the world with books that will stimulate their minds and to water the seeds of greatness inside them.*

Forever grateful,

Antoine Lunsford

Little Andy's World presents

LITTLE ANDY
RUNS FOR
SCHOOL PRESIDENT!!!

By Antoine Lunsford

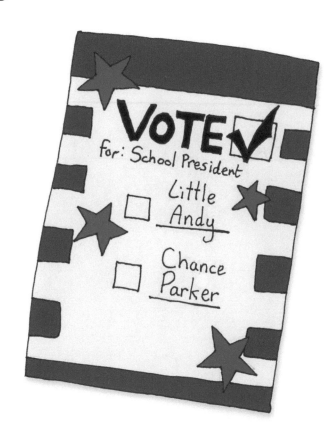

illustrated by Charity Russell

Introduction

Little Andy and Chance Parker were two of the most popular kids not only in school but also in town! They each thought that he would be a perfect fit to be school president at Spriggs Park Academy. Running for school president would create a major competition between the two of them. On one side was Chance, the son of the mayor and the superintendent, and on the other side, his opponent, Little Andy, the school recess monitor and neighborhood hero. It would be a tight race to win the title of school president. Let's find out who wins!

It was another Monday in Spriggs Park as Little Andy and his friends walked to school. They were excited to start the week.

"This week is going to be great! The football team just won our first school championship, and the morning pep rally is going to be crazy," said Little Andy.

"I can't wait to go to the pep rally!" shouted Giovanni.

"Since everybody is so excited, let's race to school, and the last person there buys everybody snacks out of the vending machine!" yelled Sammi. And they all raced to the school.

When they arrived at the front door, they noticed a huge poster on the door that read, "Run for school president! If you think you're a good leader and can help students, you'll be the perfect candidate for the job!

"Andy, you're a good leader. You should run for the position," said Frankie.

"I don't know," replied Little Andy.

"Come on, bro. You would be a great president, like George Washington or Abraham Lincoln!" shouted Jayce.

"Now that I think about it, you're right," responded Little Andy. "I should run for school president. I would be a good school president! I'm smart, I'm strong, handsome—

Giovanni interrupts him saying, "What does that have to do with anything?"

"Nothing really, but I can do the job because I'm good at helping others."

"Does that mean you're going to do it?" asked Maya.

"Do it! Do it! Do it!" his friends all screamed.

"Okay, I'll do it!" said Little Andy.

"Yes!" his friends yelled.

"It's not official until you formally announce it," said Sammi.

"Boys and girls of Spriggs Park Academy, I, Little Andy, am running for school president!" he announced.

"Yay!" all his friends cheered.

Suddenly, a long, black limousine parked in front of the school.

"Oh, no! Please don't let that be who I think it is," said Little Andy.

"I wonder who's in that limo," said Giovanni. The door of the limo opened. Everyone was so anxious to see who it was! Who could it be? they all thought. Suddenly, a red carpet rolled from out of the limousine. It was—Chance Parker, the son of Mayor Parker and Superintendent Parker!

"Aww, man. Not that guy!" Little Andy said.

"He's so cute, and his hair smells like the beach! Somebody, catch me," swooned Frankie. She fell backwards into Maya's arms, and they both giggled.

Chance walked up the stairs to the door and said, "Hey, everybody. I just got back in town from my week-long vacation in Spain, and I'm ready to run for school president. Hope you guys will vote for me."

Little Andy lowered his head and took a deep breath. Little Andy and his friends all looked at each other in fear as they walked into the school.

After lunch, the pep rally kicked off in the auditorium with the football team getting their football jackets for winning the school's first elementary school state championship in football. The students went crazy!! As the football players received their jackets, they all thanked their coaches.

Kumar, the captain of the football team, grabbed the microphone and said, "I'd like to thank Coach Brooks and all the football team staff for helping us become the best players we could be, and I want to thank my friend, Little Andy. If it weren't for you, I wouldn't have passed my reading assessment, and I would have been kicked off the team. Thanks for helping me believe in myself."

All the students cheered, "Andy! Andy! Andy!"

As they continued to cheer, Principal Thomas walked onto the stage. She seemed eager to make an announcement.

As she approached the podium, Little Andy cringed.

"Good afternoon, boys and girls," she said.

"Good afternoon, Principal Thomas," the students responded.

"Earlier today, everyone voted on who they think would be a good leader as school president. As all the votes were tallied, two names came up consistently. These two individuals will be running against each other for the title of school president. Drumroll, please." The students started making drum noises.

"The two students who will be competing against each other—Chance Parker and Little Andy!" Principal Thomas announced.

The students cheered. Both students came to the stage and shook hands.

Chance then whispered in Little Andy's ear, "May the best student win."

Little Andy took a deep breath and walked away. After school, Little Andy walked home, and his friends caught up with him.

"Andy, you haven't been acting like yourself all day," said Maya.

"I can't win. I've never beaten Chance at anything. Every time we race, he wins. When we play video games, he wins. Whether we play sports or have a hotdog eating contest, he ALWAYS wins!!" Little Andy screamed. "But this time is going to be different. I'm going to win school president! Even though Principal Thomas said we can't start campaigning until Friday, that's more than enough time for us to put our heads together and come up with some cool ideas to get students to vote for me. Do you guys have time to meet me at the library to come up with a few ideas?"

"Yes!" his friends all shouted, following Little Andy to the library to figure out how they could help him.

Friday is finally here, and everyone is excited! Throughout the day, Little Andy and his friends tell students to meet him after school at Igloo's Ice Cream Parlor for free ice cream to hear a speech about why he'd be a great school president. After the school day, everyone rushed to the ice cream parlor! After all the students received their two free scoops of ice cream and were seated, Little Andy was ready to give his speech.

"Good afternoon, boys and girls. I'm so glad you could make it here. I think I will be a good school president because—"

Before Little Andy could finish his sentence, Chance pushed open the doors of the ice cream parlor and yelled through his bullhorn, "Hey, everybody! If you want to hear what I would do as school president, come over to my mansion for my pool party and cookout!"

All the kids looked at Little Andy and immediately ran out of the ice cream parlor all the way to Chance's mansion. Chance then looked at Little Andy with a grin on his face and walked out.

"Did he really just do that?" asked Giovanni.

"He did, and I'm not surprised," said Little Andy.

"I say we go over there and tell Chance what he did was wrong in front of all the students, and that might cause them to leave," said Sammi.

"That's a good idea, Sammi. You guys go ahead. I'm going to clean up. When I'm done, I'll be right there," said Little Andy.

His friends ran out as fast as they could.

When Little Andy arrived at Chance's mansion, he couldn't believe his eyes. He saw all his friends playing in the swimming pool!

He quickly ran to the gate and said, "Guys! What are you doing?"

"Hey, Little Andy," they all replied.

"I thought you were going to tell Chance in front of everybody that he was wrong for what he did," Little Andy said.

"We did," said Frankie. "After we told him, he apologized, and then he gave us all this food and water balloons!" said Jayce.

Chance then walked over to the gate where Little Andy was and said, "Little Andy! Come in and enjoy the party."

"No, thanks," Little Andy responded. "Guys, I'll see you Monday at school," he said and sadly walked home.

On Monday, Little Andy was excited to tell all the students why he would be a good school president. At lunch, he met with his friends.

"Guys, our plan worked! Last week before school was out, I asked Principal Thomas if I could have an ad in the school paper, the Spriggs Park Express, and she said yes!"

"That's great, Little Andy. So, what's the next step in the plan?" asked Maya.

"After school, we're going to split into teams around the school and pass out the papers. Giovanni and Maya, you'll pass out papers to the students as they get on the school bus. Frankie and Jayce, you'll be on the corner to pass out papers to walkers and car riders. Kumar and Sammi, you'll pass out papers at the side door exit, and I'll pass out papers in front of the school. Are you guys ready?"

"Yeah!" his friends shouted.

They went to their positions and passed out the papers. As students walked by them, they would say, "Vote for Little Andy. He'll be the best school president ever!!" Or "are you tired of eating that nasty school lunch? Vote for Little Andy. He'll change that!" And "are you tired of getting a lot of homework and not enough time to play at recess? Vote for Little Andy, and you'll work less and play more!"

The students were excited to see their favorite recess monitor in the school newspaper! Little Andy and his friends were able to pass out all the newspapers! They briefly met afterwards in front of the school to talk.

"Thank you all so much for your help. Let's celebrate with some steak and cheese subs from Frita's Sub Shack."

"Let's do it!" all his friends cheered as they raced off.

As Little Andy walked home, people waved at him, honked their horns, and yelled, "Little Andy, you'll be a great school president!"
It made Little Andy feel good—until he got home.

When Little Andy arrived home, he walked in to speak to his family. But before he could speak, a newsflash appeared on the television.

"Good evening. Welcome to the Spriggs Park four o'clock news. I'm your host, Brad Bell. Tonight, I'm reporting to you live from the Spriggs Park Town Hall with breaking news: Mayor Parker is running for re-election! Mayor Parker, would you please come and say a few words?"

Mayor Parker walked in front of the camera with Chance by his side!

"Hello, good citizens of Spriggs Park! I, Mayor Parker, am running for re-election for mayor, but more importantly, my son Chance is running for school president. I hope all the students at Spriggs Park Academy will support him," he said.

All the children in the background cheered, "Chance! Chance! Chance! Chance! Chance!"

Little Andy couldn't believe it.

"He's on TV! I can't out do that! But it's okay. I've got one more trick up my sleeve, and on Friday, everyone will be surprised," Little Andy said as he raced upstairs to his room.

After he planned for the past few days, it was finally Friday, and Little Andy was excited! He decided to arrive at school a little earlier to meet with his friends.

When he arrived, all he could say was "I'm ready to become school president!!"

"Did you ask Principal Thomas about our idea?" asked Frankie.

"I did, and guess what? She approved it!" he shouted.

"Yes!" his friends screamed.

"After school we are going to have a video game night in the multi-purpose room. All we have to do is give Principal Thomas our money, and she's going to order the pizza for us. Ms. Manetti and Ms. Phillips are setting up all the video games for us now!" yelled Little Andy.

"Tonight is going to be so much fun," said Giovanni.

"I can't wait," said Jayce.

Finally, after hours of anticipation, the final school bell rang for dismissal, and the students raced to the multi-purpose room excited! They were playing video games, eating, and playing games on their tablets and laptops.

Little Andy was ready to tell everyone why he'd be a great school president when Chance ran into the room with his bullhorn and shouted, "Hey, everybody! My parents rented out the Spriggs Park Movie Theater for me tonight! I'm inviting all of you to see *Superheroes 6*, and the best part is all the food is included! You can eat all the popcorn, hotdogs, and nachos you want along with all the soda refills and candy you can eat! If you're ready for a real night of fun, follow me!"

Chance then raced out of the door.

All the students looked at Little Andy and then raced out of the doors behind Chance.

Little Andy couldn't believe it!

"Sorry, Little Andy. I know you wanted this event to work," said Frankie.

"Guys, I'm really disappointed!" said Little Andy.

"Do you want us to stay and help you clean up?" asked Sammi.

"No. You guys should go to the movies with all of the kids. You all have been wanting to see *Superheroes 6* since the beginning of the school year.

They all looked at Little Andy and said, "See you later," and they raced out the door to the movie theater.

Monday, school president election day, was here, and Little Andy felt so sad.

As he walked to school, he said to himself, "I thought I could win" over and over. As he got closer to the school, he started to notice flyers with his face on them on light posts, buildings, trees and trash cans! How could this be? As he stood in disbelief, his friends approached him.

"Did you guys do this?" asked Little Andy.

"We did," they responded. "Our parents let us stay out a little longer on Sunday and put all these flyers out," said Kumar.

"We want you to win," said Maya.

"Thanks, guys. I feel really confident that I'll win today," replied Little Andy.

As they continued to walk to school, Jayce noticed something in the air.

"What's that?" asked Jayce as everyone looked up in awe!

"You have *got* to be kidding me!" groaned Little Andy.

What was it in the sky? It was an airplane flying through the sky with a banner on it that read, "Vote for Chance Parker for school president!"

"I should have known this was going to happen. I thought just one time I could beat Chance at something, but I can't," Little Andy muttered.

"It's not over, Little Andy!" yelled Maya.

"You're going to win," said Giovanni.

"We're not going to let you lose Little Andy," shouted Jayce.

All those kind words made Little Andy smile and feel confident again. They then walked into the building, ready to vote!

Twelve o'clock! Students from all grade levels came into the multipurpose room to vote. Chance and Little Andy shouted, "Vote for me!" as each class went in. At the end of the day, the teachers counted the votes and placed them behind the stage in the storage room. As students were leaving to go home, Little Andy remembered he left his bookbag in the multipurpose room by the stage. When he went back to get it, he heard noises coming from behind the stage. He went to see what was happening. As he got closer to the door of the storage room, he heard laughing and the sound of paper being ripped. When he opened the door, he froze. He couldn't believe his eyes! Giovanni and Jayce were ripping up votes!

"How could you guys do this?!" Little Andy yelled.

"We wanted you to win," said Jayce. "We knew it meant a lot to you to beat Chance at something, so we wanted to make sure you won for once," replied Giovanni.

"I want to win, but not like this. Hurry up and get out of here. I'll fix this," said Little Andy.

"Sorry, bro," said Jayce.

"I'm really sorry, too," said Giovanni.

After they both apologized, they left. Little Andy wondered what he could do to fix this.

"I got it. All I have to do is rip up as many votes as I can with my name on them, and hopefully that will give Chance more votes," he said.

As he started to rip up the votes with his name on it, a huge shadow loomed over him. It was Principal Thomas!!

"Little Andy, what are you doing?" she asked with a firm voice.

"It's not what you think," he responded.

"It's exactly what I think it is. You're ripping up votes so that you can win. I never thought that you'd do something like this. As of right now, you will be in after-school detention for a week!" she scolded.

"But Principal Thomas—" he said.

"I don't want to hear it. Go home, Little Andy," she yelled.

Little Andy then walked off the stage and out of the building, wondering how he would explain this to his parents.

When Little Andy arrived home, he sat on his front porch with his head down. As soon as his parents saw him, they came outside to check on him.

"What's wrong, Son?" Dad asked.

"I can't do anything right," said Little Andy.

"That's not true," said Mom. "You do a lot of things right."

"It doesn't seem like it," Little Andy responded.

"What's on your mind, Son?" Dad asked.

"Today, I saw Jayce and Giovanni ripping up votes with Chance's name on them so I can win. I told them that I didn't want to win that way, so I started ripping up votes with my name on them to try to even things out, but Principal Thomas caught me, and now I'm going to be in after-school detention for a week," he cried.

"Don't worry, Son. I understand that you're upset. Everything will work out," said Dad.

"I'm sure your friends will do the right thing and confess. You're too good of a friend to let down. If your friends really cared, they'll make sure Principal Thomas knows the truth," said Mom. "Why don't you go upstairs and relax for a little bit and give them a call later?"

"That's a great idea! I think I'll do that!" Little Andy responded as he walked into the house.

After a few hours of rest, he decided to call Giovanni, but no one picked up. He then called Jayce's house. Again, no one picked up.

"They must be avoiding me. I can't believe these guys! They're supposed to be my friends!" Little Andy groaned. "Would they really let me take the blame for this?"

He drifted off to sleep wondering what was going to happen tomorrow.

As Little Andy woke up the next morning, he was not excited about going to school. Today, not only did his week-long after-school detention start, but it was also the day that Principal Thomas would announce who the school president would be. As soon as Little Andy arrived for school, Principal Thomas called him into her office for a meeting.

"Little Andy, I'm cancelling your detention," she said.

"Really? I mean, thank you!" he said.

"Before you arrived, Jayce and Giovanni came into my office and explained everything to me. I apologize for not letting you tell me your side of the story," said Principal Thomas.

"It's okay," replied Little Andy.

"Now it's time for me to announce the school president. Follow me to the multipurpose room," she said.

Little Andy followed with his head down.

"There's no way I won, but at least I tried," he said to himself.

Principal Thomas walked onto the stage to make the announcement. Everyone was so excited!

The students cheered back and forth: "Let's go, Andy!" "Let's go, Chance!" "Let's go, Andy!" "Let's go, Chance!"

"Good morning! Welcome to our school president rally!"

The students cheered.

"It's time to announce the winner of our school president race. Thank you, Chance and Little Andy, for your participation and for all the campaigning you've done. Now, the moment you've all been waiting for!"

The students all stood to their feet.

The winner of this year's school president race is—Chance Parker!!" she shouted.

All the students chanted, "Chance! Chance! Chance! Chance!"

Chance walked onto the stage, and Principal Thomas handed him the microphone.

"Thank you to everyone who voted for me and to my parents who helped me campaign. Truthfully, I'm not a good leader. I just try to do fun things so everyone will like me. I ran for school president because I wanted attention from my parents. They're always busy working and don't have time for me. I knew that if I ran for school president, they'd help me run, and I really enjoyed just having all their attention for a change. So, I think Little Andy should be school president," Chance said as he ran off stage and jumped into the arms of his parents.

Little Andy went on stage, and Principal Thomas, surprised, handed him the microphone: "Thank you, Chance, for giving me the title of school president, but you won the race fair and square. So, I'll be your vice president and help you be a good leader and make some new friends."

Chance ran back on stage and cheered, "Let's do it!"

They then raised each other's hands in victory, and the students cheered!

THE END

LITTLE ANDY'S WORLD: CHARACTER BIOGRAPHIES

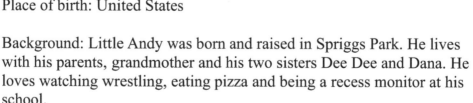

Character: Little Andy

Full name: Andy Langford

Age: 12

Place of birth: United States

Background: Little Andy was born and raised in Spriggs Park. He lives with his parents, grandmother and his two sisters Dee Dee and Dana. He loves watching wrestling, eating pizza and being a recess monitor at his school.

Character: Jayce aka DJ Fast Fingers

Full name: Jayce Yi

Age: 11

Place of birth: Beijing, China

Background: Jayce was born in Beijing, China. At age 8, his mother decided to move the United States to start her own clothing business. She thought Spriggs Park was a beautiful town so she moved her and Jayce there. Jayce likes to play basketball, perform as a DJ at school parties and drink chocolate milk.

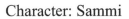

Character: Sammi

Full name: Sammi Lovato-Styles

Age: 11

Place of birth: United States

Background: Sammi was born in Newark, New Jersey. She was raised by her Aunt. Her aunt found a better job and relocated them to Spriggs Park to be closer to her new job. Sammi loves to play baseball, football, soccer, and lacrosse.

Character: Giovanni

Full name: Giovanni Alvarez

Age: 11

Place of birth: Mexico City, Mexico

Background: Giovanni's dad is in the military. After a few years of living in Mexico, his parents relocated the family to a military base in Spriggs Park. Giovanni loves fishing, painting, swimming, juggling, and running.

Character: Frankie

Full name: Frankie Chapman

Age: 11

Place of birth: United States

Background: Frankie was born in Lakeland, Florida. At age 9, her parents decided to move the family from Florida to Spriggs Park. She likes to shop for dresses, eat cheeseburgers and play the violin.

Character: Maya

Full name: Maya Anderson

Age:11

Place of birth: United States

Background: Maya lived with her dad in Baltimore. Her dad was raised in Spriggs Park and wanted to Maya to grow up there too. He also owns the best Ice cream business in town called Igloo's Ice Cream Parlor. Maya loves painting her nails, cheerleading, eating sushi and dressing her dogs up in outfits.

Character: Kumar

Full name: Kumar Mahal

Age: 11

Place of birth: Mumbai, India

Background: Kumar was born in India. His family moved to New York City and then to Spriggs Park because they thought it would be a great place to live.

A Message from the Author

Always give your best effort. Even if you do come up short, no one can say you didn't try. Not trying to so something is the worst you can do. You'll never know what could have happened or what you could have learned in that moment. In other words,

Quitters never win, and winners never quit!

Give your best in everything you do, and expect good things to happen!

With love,

Antoine Lunsford

CPSIA information can be obtained
at www.ICGtesting.com
Printed in the USA
LVHW011223061019
633320LV00004B/61/P